Dear Parents:

Congratulations! Your child is taking the first steps on an exciting journey. The destination? Independent reading!

STEP INTO READING® will help your child get there. The program offers five steps to reading success. Each step includes fun stories and colorful art or photographs. In addition to original fiction and books with favorite characters, there are Step into Reading Non-Fiction Readers, Phonics Readers and Boxed Sets, Sticker Readers, and Comic Readers—a complete literacy program with something to interest every child.

Learning to Read, Step by Step!

Ready to Read   Preschool–Kindergarten
• big type and easy words • rhyme and rhythm • picture clues
For children who know the alphabet and are eager to begin reading.

Reading with Help   Preschool–Grade 1
• basic vocabulary • short sentences • simple stories
For children who recognize familiar words and sound out new words with help.

Reading on Your Own   Grades 1–3
• engaging characters • easy-to-follow plots • popular topics
For children who are ready to read on their own.

Reading Paragraphs   Grades 2–3
• challenging vocabulary • short paragraphs • exciting stories
For newly independent readers who read simple sentences with confidence.

Ready for Chapters   Grades 2–4
• chapters • longer paragraphs • full-color art
For children who want to take the plunge into chapter books but still like colorful pictures.

STEP INTO READING® is designed to give every child a successful reading experience. The grade levels are only guides; children will progress through the steps at their own speed, developing confidence in their reading.

Remember, a lifetime love of reading starts with a single step!

Visit us on the Web!
StepIntoReading.com
randomhousekids.com

Educators and librarians, for a variety of teaching tools, visit us at RHTeachersLibrarians.com

ISBN 978-0-7364-3338-9 (trade) — ISBN 978-0-7364-8224-0 (lib. bdg.)
ISBN 978-0-7364-3339-6 (ebook)

Printed in the United States of America 10 9 8 7 6 5 4 3 2 1

FIRE 🔥 CREW!

by Frank Berrios

illustrated by the Disney Storybook Art Team

Random House 🏠 New York

Blade Ranger is
a rescue helicopter.

He is the leader
of a fire and rescue crew!

Dusty Crophopper is
a racing champ.

He wants to become
a firefighter for
the fire crew.

Lil' Dipper is
a super-scooper.
She scoops up water
to put out fires.

Windlifter is
a heavy-lift helicopter.
He can pick up
dozens of trees!

Cabbie is a cargo plane.
He drops the
smokejumpers.

Dynamite is the leader
of the smokejumpers.

They work together
to battle the blaze
on the ground!

Pinecone uses his
bucket to push
trees and shrubs
away from the fire.

Blackout uses
his saw
to cut down trees
near the fire.

Drip lifts trees
out of the way
with his grabber claw.

Avalanche is
a bulldozer.
He clears a path
through the blaze.

Maru is a mechanic.
He can fix
almost anything!

Patch works at
the control tower.
She keeps a lookout
for new fires.

Pulaski is a fire truck.
He works at the hotel
in Piston Peak
National Park.

Ol' Jammer is
a park ranger
in Piston Peak.
He knows everything
about the park!

Dusty is proud to be
the newest member
of the fire crew!